A NOTE TO PARENTS

Reading Aloud with Your Child

Research shows that reading books aloud is the single most valuable support parents can provide in helping children learn to read.

- Be a ham! The more enthusiasm you display, the more your child will enjoy the book.
- Run your finger underneath the words as you read to signal that the print carries the story.
- Leave time for examining the illustrations more closely; encourage your child to find things in the pictures.
- Invite your youngster to join in whenever there's a repeated phrase in the text.
- Link up events in the book with similar events in your child's life.
- If your child asks a question, stop and answer it. The book can be a means to learning more about your child's thoughts.

Listening to Your Child Read Aloud

The support of your attention and praise is absolutely crucial to your child's continuing efforts to learn to read.

- If your child is learning to read and asks for a word, give it immediately so that the meaning of the story is not interrupted. DO NOT ask your child to sound out the word.
- On the other hand, if your child initiates the act of sounding out, don't intervene.
- If your child is reading along and makes what is called a miscue, listen for the sense of the miscue. If the word "road" is substituted for the word "street," for instance, no meaning is lost. Don't stop the reading for a correction.
- If the miscue makes no sense (for example, "horse" for "house"), ask your child to reread the sentence because you're not sure you understand what's just been read.
- Above all else, enjoy your child's growing command of print and make sure you give lots of praise. *You are your child's first teacher — and the most important one. Praise from you is critical for further risk-taking and learning.*

— Priscilla Lynch
Ph.D., New York University
Educational Consultant

To Jordan
— G.M.

For my dentist,
Dr. Dan Epstein
— B.L.

Text copyright © 1995 by Grace Maccarone.
Illustrations copyright © 1995 by Betsy Lewin.
All rights reserved. Published by Scholastic Inc.
HELLO READER! and CARTWHEEL BOOKS
are registered trademarks of Scholastic Inc.

Library of Congress Cataloging-in-Publication Data

Maccarone, Grace.
    My tooth is about to fall out / by Grace Maccarone : illustrated by Betsy Lewin.
        p.   cm. — (Hello reader!)
    "Level 1."
    Summary: A little girl loses a tooth.
    ISBN 0-590-48376-5
    [1.   Teeth — Fiction.]   I. Lewin, Betsy, ill.   II. Title.
    III. Series.
    PZ7.M1257My   1995
    [E] — dc20   94-9772
                                                                      CIP
                                                                       AC

25 24 23   9/9

                        Printed in the U.S.A.   24
              First Scholastic printing, February 1995

My Tooth Is About to Fall Out

by Grace Maccarone
Illustrated by Betsy Lewin

Hello Reader! — Level 1

SCHOLASTIC INC.

Cartwheel B·O·O·K·S ®

New York   Toronto   London   Auckland   Sydney

Uh-oh!
It wobbles.
It wiggles.
It joggles.
It jiggles.
My tooth
is about
to fall out.

I hope it doesn't fall
while I am playing ball

or swimming
in the pool

or having
fun at school.
But most of all,

I hope it doesn't fall
into my meatball
or in my spaghetti.

Oops!
It's already
gone!

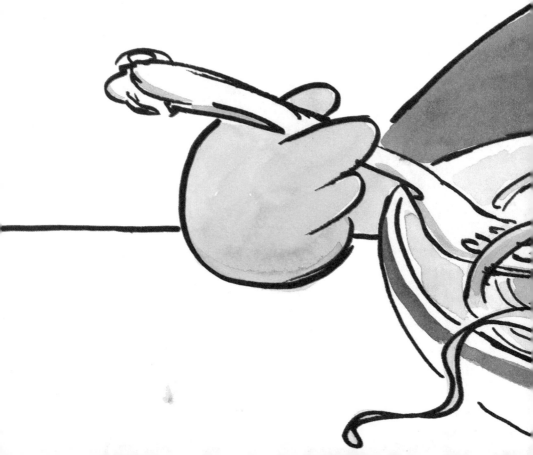

My tooth is
in my bowl.

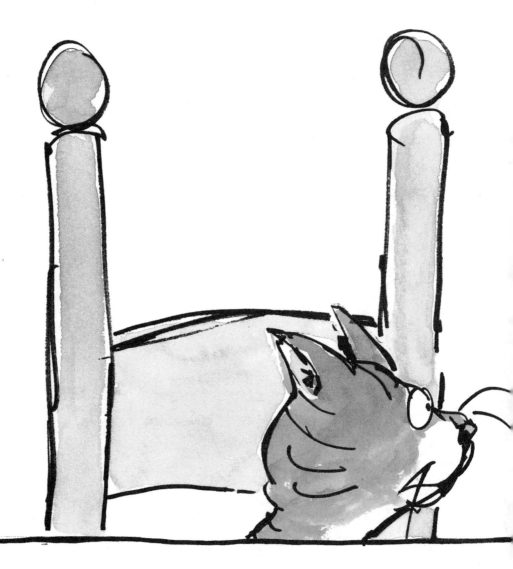

My tongue
can feel the hole.

It feels funny.
Nothing's there.
My tongue slides through.
There's only air.

Now that space
gives my face
a brand-new,
big-kid smile.

Then tonight I'll
go to sleep.
And the Tooth Fairy
will creep
into my room.

She'll take my baby tooth,
and maybe,
if I'm lucky,
she will leave
something behind
for me to find.

I had twenty
baby teeth—
with big ones
growing underneath.

My roots, I think,
dissolve and shrink
until they're small.
And so my teeth
get loose and fall.

My big teeth will
begin to show
from under my gums,
way below.

I can't wait
to see them.
They'll look
great!

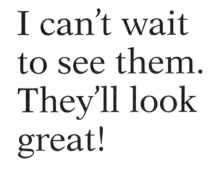